Purple Snowflakes
by h.e. newell

Copyright © 2022 h.e. newell.

All rights reserved. No part of this publication may be reproduced, distributed, or transmitted, in any form or by any means, including photocopying, recording, or other electronic or mechanical methods, without the prior written permission of the author, except in the case of brief quotations embodied in critical reviews and certain other noncommercial uses permitted by copyright law. For permission requests, write to

throneroomjewel@gmail.com

Any references to historical events, real people, or places are used fictitiously. Names, characters, and places are products of the author's imagination.

Book Layout © 2016 BookDesignTemplates.com

Tree of Life (TLV) Translation of the Bible. Copyright © 2015 by The Messianic Jewish Family Bible Society.

Dedication

For You, King Jesus. My husband, my friend, my redeemer. Without You I would still be a slave to anguish, self-hate, and anxiety. Your presence is the sweetest.

For my girls, the strongest, most beautiful people I know. You have inspired me to be a better person from the moment I knew you were growing inside me.

Thank you, Sheri, for walking this out with me...for always being more than my sister-in-law. Thank you for believing in me when I couldn't believe in myself.

For my other self. I have loved you before I even knew you. I'm excited to enjoy the goodness of the Lord in the Land of the Living with you.

Cover Art

Untitled by M. Kerbo

Psalm 68:15 (TLV)

When *Shaddai* scattered kings there,
it was snowing on Zalmon.

Dancing Alone...
(19 January 2005)

catching
soft
cool
perfect...
dances on the wind
harmonies...

unique love falling
kissing my face
cheeks, chin, eyes...
rest in my hair like pearls
only for a moment
before you melt like wax

raise my hands to the One
who sends the promises.
Promise Maker
Promise Keeper
tiny flakes touch my hands
like a lover...
here is love
dancing with me

around me
melting on me
refreshing this sleeping heart

what music is there?
what sound can describe the magic?
there is none
silence speaks loudly, clearly
smiles shine

this is the dance of
a thousand ages
the joy of the ageless One
deep within me
footprints circle in the white, soft...
manna? feathers?
who could feel the cold
when the dance is so deep...
manna falls on my tongue...
feathers fall on my face...
miracles surround me

like falling stars,
i catch as many as i can.
my spirit holding each one close.

put them in my alabaster box
until i pour them out for the one...
the only one...

here they are!
the tears which followed my prayers...
returned to me
no longer bitter...
but made sweetly perfect

Contents

Dedication — 3

Dancing Alone — 5

Marvin Gaye & gas station coffee... — 11

Psalm 23 — 19

Purple Snowflakes — 21

Write About It — 101

Psalm 139:16 (TLV)

16 Your eyes saw me when I was unformed,
and in Your book were written the days that were formed—
when not one of them had come to be.

11 Purple Snowflakes

Marvin Gaye and gas station coffee...

In June 2019, two years and a month after being life flighted one hundred miles to Pittsburgh..., my shop burned down.

Well, not just my shop; my shop and four apartments. In a historical building. In a small town on a Saturday morning. My shop, lovingly named The Copper Flamingo after my Nan's kitchen. My shop that I spent my inheritance to build, very likely without wisdom and outside of God's plan for my life, with my youngest daughter.

My shop...
I remember it all in a sort of slow motion, out of body, distorted Matrix-like scene.

We slept in the halotherapy room because we were working late making soap. Early the next morning, I sat at the desk waiting for oil to heat for the next batch. Suddenly smoke. The alarm blaring. Falling on the floor and shouting for Ahava to get out.

To this day we swear it was an angel helping me get up so I could run outside.

The crowd gathering on the street, firefighters everywhere, the landlord shouting in my face, the girl who owned the tanning salon next door biting her nails, one of my vendors blowing up my phone...and my livelihood, my life, Ahava's new dance costume...going up in flames.

Me standing there helpless, strangely numb, telling God, "I will rejoice and praise Your name, no matter what happens. I refuse to be defeated. You are all I need."

Michelle coming suddenly up the street and taking Ahava home with her. Sam hugging me for dear life when she found me in the crowd. Leslie hobbling through the people... How God showed me He was present through them.

I remember that night...going home to a swirling vortex of dysfunction in addition to being in shock. When everyone finally went to bed, the silence was maddening. Ahava couldn't be away from me for more than a few minutes, and the smell of smoke made the both of us panic.

I remember going through the motions for the next five weeks. The gracious and the ungracious around me. The insurance company who fought for me, the landlord who wanted to sue me for over 2 million dollars, the vendor whose mental illness drove her to lambast me to whoever would listen, the friends who quietly tried to help while they worried for my mental health, the friends we made when we began to go to church again, the kids' school who sued me for back tuition knowing I had nothing.

I remember how I began to fade into despair as I watched us fall deeper into poverty. My credit worse than ever... I feared that I had broken the vow I made as I watched the shop burn down.

I remember the day there was nothing left to live on, so I began to feed horses for a woman who was notoriously difficult to work for. She found ways to short my pay every week. Diana bought me barn boots (which I still love). Nicole would meet me for coffee on my way home sometimes.

I remember how it was -22 degrees in the mornings. I would talk to Holy Spirit while chiseling out the van at 4:30 am. I would praise on the twenty-five-minute drive to the farm. Feeding the horses became therapy. The biggest horse on the farm was my favourite, and I was his. His name was Scout and he liked apple snacks and peppermints. The rudest horse in the lower stable loved me, and I loved him. His name was Cole, and no one else could turn him out when I was there.

I remember Christmas morning there were little cards with my name on them on certain stalls. Including Scout and Cole's. I remember thinking how precious that the horse owners knew my name. How the twenty

15 Purple Snowflakes

dollars in the envelope could fill the tank. How twenty in the other could buy dog food and toilet paper. I had every penny in these envelopes designated before I opened the next one. I was living so low, it felt like I had a million dollars.

I remember driving home, remembering that Sheetz had free coffee on Christmas, and deciding to get petrol there. I stepped out of the van and heard my favourite Christmas song, "Purple Snowflakes".

Love washed over me as soon as my feet touched the ground.

I listened to every velvety word, every beautiful sentiment, every delicate sound of that song and felt Jesus in all of it. I felt hope well up inside of me again, knowing 2020 would be a fresh beginning. I felt joy knowing that my family was safe and together in our tiny little mobile home. I felt peace knowing that no matter how stressful or horrible things could be, God always provides.

I needed that, because in my flesh I struggled with having so many people to take care of, feeling like a failure, and not allowing people to help me. Prior to 2019, my life had become a pattern of painfully learning that I could only rely on God and myself. Now I needed to get me out of the equation. But there were so many memories and years of everything being on me, I didn't even know who I was. I was shutting down.

A story began ruminating in my thoughts.

I took the long way home, around the lake and back through the Amish part of the county. I wondered, "What could it be like if I just had the opportunity to get quiet?" What would happen if I just shut down and stopped everything...? How glorious it would be to be able to focus on Jesus only, to give Him all of it so it wouldn't hurt so much anymore.

I mean He works it all out for my good, right?

That very day, I began to write this story, and it has evolved with me. Every time He sets me free of something, I edit it. Every time I walk out forgiving someone, I edit it. Every time He redeems a moment, I edit it.

17   Purple Snowflakes

Every time I hear the song "Purple Snowflakes", I embrace the love and joy it evokes in me, the memory of so many winters where everything was covered in sparkling snow. Everything was possible, everything was pure.

Some of this story is autobiographical. Some of it is a quiet embellishment of people and times I have known. Some of it may prophesy what I believe the future holds. Writers weave everything together, you see, as we ask the question, "What if?" Our sacrifice and our redemption are in every word we write.

In this moment, I can't say that I have recovered everything I lost in the fire. I haven't recovered everything I lost before that. I might never. I'm sure I'm not meant to, because some of what we lose in life we were never meant to have in the first place. I've become okay with that.

What I have gained since I stood barefoot in the street on a warm June morning in a sleepy Pennsylvania town as my shop burned down, is beyond anything I could have imagined. Every day, it becomes deeper, more beautiful, literally miraculous.

   Every day this song means even more to me.

   We are surely blessed.

Adonai-Ro-eh   (TLV)

Psalm 23

¹ A psalm of David.
Adonai is my shepherd, I shall not want.
² He makes me lie down in green pastures.
He leads me beside still waters.
³ He restores my soul.
He guides me in paths of righteousness
    for His Name's sake.

⁴ Even though I walk through the valley of the shadow of death,
I will fear no evil, for You are with me:
Your rod and Your staff comfort me.
⁵ You prepare a table before me in the presence of my enemies.
You have anointed my head with oil, my cup overflows.
⁶ Surely goodness and mercy will follow me all the days of my life,
and I will dwell in the House
of *Adonai* forever.

h.e. newell   20

21 Purple Snowflakes

I

My grandson brings me a paper snowflake and a frosted sugar cookie he knows I'll never eat.
He does this almost daily.

My bedroom door is covered in paper snowflakes he's made with his siblings,
but he saves the window for the incredibly special ones.
Like this one, still damp with white school glue.
It's covered in a thick layer of purple iridescent glitter, with a tiny green pompom glued to the almost center.
I watch as he moves yesterday's snowflake to make room for this new masterpiece, carefully peeling the tape away with his thumbnail.

His hazel eyes are sparkling blue today.
They match the snowflake he brought me last Wednesday.
He has the most beautiful smile as he turns to me and climbs onto my lap.
With a soft creak,
my rocking chair responds to his added weight and movement.
Then he invites himself under my blanket,
wrapping himself in my arms.

Oh! His soft little hands are so warm.
I'm sure he is anointed for healing,
for deliverance.
He curls an arm around my neck and plays with my hair with one hand.
the other he leaves on my cheek.
This boy melts me.
I remember how he stole my heart the moment he was born.

I remember a lot of things.
Things; moments, hours, victories, failures, adventures, mishaps, traumas,
I don't just remember.
No, I re-experience them
as though they're happening all over again.

23 Purple Snowflakes

There's just so much.
My entire life seems to have been a fight for so many years.
Some of it might have killed me without God.
He has numbered my days, though,
and I have triumphed over more than I will ever know.
Now I'm just trying to file everything...

It's a simple enough system.
Forgive.
Forget.
Treasure.
Trash.
I just had to get quiet so I could sort through it all.

I want to become a quiet place.
I don't want to be dwelling in the pain and negativity from the past,
I want to dwell in the tents of the Lord and think on the lovely things.

Today is the seven hundred and sixty-fourth day since I stopped speaking.
Talk is cheap.
I had nothing left.

Not even for my husband, who, apart from being the most beautiful man I have ever met,
   is the gentlest soul I know.
   Of all people, he would have listened...
   but I was too exhausted.
   I could not pretend I was okay any longer.
   I felt as though I was just adding to the noise around me.

   So. I. Just. Stopped. Speaking.

   Looking back, I wonder that I shouldn't have stopped years before.
   Perhaps if I had, someone might have noticed and given me a reprieve.
   Absolution.
   Clemency in place of the harsh punishment I gave myself for simply living,
   for making so many mistakes,
   for the tumultuous life my children had.
   Maybe something might have shifted sooner.
   My confession might have brought life and not death.
   But people are not responsible for the condition of my soul.
   No one can walk out my healing and deliverance but me

and my Deliverer.

Seven hundred and sixty-four days ago, I admitted that I was weary and made myself rest.
I finally trusted my Shepherd enough to willingly lay down in the meadow.
We've been beside quiet waters ever since.
Resting.
Processing.
Working out forgiveness.
Sometimes I even forgive myself.
My soul is being restored.

"Pretty purple snowflakes...," this boy sings.
I taught him this song when he was four.
Just like my mother taught me.

"We're surely blessed..."
He has a voice like a lark.
Just like his mother.
Funny, someone once said that about me when I was his age.

But this boy does,
and he is singing my favourite Christmas song, by one of my favourite singers,
while snuggled up under my favourite blanket, in what could be my favourite chair.

I used to dance when he sang songs with me, for me, to me...
Now we just rock in front of the window.
I don't think I mind.
I mean...

Purple Snowflakes

II

I remember the day they brought the rocking chair into my room,
  fifty-seven days before I got quiet,
  as though it is happening now.

  A warm Friday morning.
  My cardboard breakfast untouched on the bedside table.
  My son in law sets the cable rocking chair on the floor in front of the window.
  He's a nice young man; he's pretended to tolerate me for years.
  My oldest daughter kisses me on the cheek and says I look nice.
  Perhaps I do; she wouldn't lie.
  She tells me that I love rocking chairs as she ties a purple cushion to the seat.

  "You have since you were a little girl, Mommy," she says,

trying to hide the desperation in her voice.

She looks to my husband for encouragement.
He suggests she gives me a moment.
I sit down.
The cushions smell of sandalwood and vanilla.

She holds a picture up for me to look at. I'm about four years old,
wearing a sombrero,
sitting in my grandmother's rocker and smiling.
Then another.
I'm a teenager.
Black eyeliner, shaved hair, and my neurologically impaired aunt sits on my lap.
We're singing her favourite nursery rhyme, smiling.
Still another.
I'm twenty-two, smiling in some sad way.
"Is that me you're pregnant with?"
She knows it is.
And a last one.
She's with her sister, in matching pink dresses, in my grandmother's rocker with their great-great Nana.

They're young, four and six, and smiling.
Nana died a few years later.
That was four hundred and twelve days before...
She wants me to remember,
smiling in my grandmother's rocking chair...
but she doesn't understand.

I remember how horribly that woman treated me when I was pregnant,
and how hateful she was to this sweet girl when she was only a child.
This woman who knew a different Jesus than I did.

I remember the day, six thousand nine hundred and thirty-five days ago,
when Children's Services showed up at the house because my family called them.
I remember vomiting in the kitchen sink when the worker told me what had been said.
So utterly confused.
I remember how my girls swore that no one was touching them.
I remember how our lives changed that morning.

My mother was on a plane that night.
The man who abused me when we were married continued to threaten to kill me and steal my children,
because my family somehow found him and told him where I was.

I remember how miserable my sweet girls were for years,
and how I didn't understand why...

Until I found out it was true three thousand six hundred and eighty-eight days later...

I remember screaming in the garage when the kids went to bed that night.
I remember sobbing on the phone to my mother...
I remember hating those family members all over again, after fighting so hard to forgive them.
I remember thinking how different things could have been for my girls if only someone had told *me,*
rather than telling other people that I knew and didn't care.
I remember moments and incidents over the years that made more sense now

and I feel like a failure.

I remember the very second when I accepted that I was indeed the horrible, lacking mother that too many people to list told me I was.

I remember the hours I spent talking to Jesus about all of it,
how He reminded me of my identity,
how He healed us.
I remember how He helped me forgive those family members,
how He held me close and helped me forgive myself.

How Holy Spirit walked me through redeeming my ancestors and breaking curses and soul ties.
How I cried out for God to take the scales from my eyes...
to restore me to the place where I could see people with His eyes again.
He always gives good gifts.
He answered my cries and helped me see how broken my grandmother was...

I remember the day my God told my husband to tell me I was a good mother.

It healed something deeper than even I had remembered.
He was only my friend at the time,
but I knew in that moment I couldn't do life without him.

All stirred up by pictures of a rocking chair.

And then my daughter apologizes because the rocking chair she bought me isn't just like my grandmother's.
But...I smile at that.
"Thank God!" I want to shout.
Because I've realized that I hate that rocking chair in the pictures and what it represents.
"I hope to Heaven they forget to give it to me when she dies!" I want to scream.
But instead, I smile and quietly say, "This is wonderful, Booboolah."
At least... I think it is.
I know I love rocking chairs; I just don't want to remember *that* one.

No, I decide to remember that this one is just like the one her father brought home a week before she was born.
How happy he was for a moment.

How much I loved nursing her and her younger sister in that chair,
rocking them to sleep in it even after he left.
Oddly, I don't remember what happened to it or when it disappeared,
only that all I had to nurse their baby sister in was a broken lawn chair.

"Come sit with me," I invite.
She does.
I tell her about the old rocking chair for the first time.
She needs to hear a new story.
Something redeeming about her father.
We make a new memory.
She smiles that dazzling smile, her eyes twinkle.
My husband strokes my hair and I feel perfectly still.
That was eight hundred and twenty-one days ago.

III

   Today, while this boy tells me all about his day at the skating rink, his mother puts the laundry away.

   She does this for my husband, she says, to make caring for me easier.
   When I first stopped leaving the house, I wore the same pajamas for four days.
   The kids worried, the grandchildren thought I was sick and went into a panic...
   The girls asked me to "at least get dressed every other day".
   I love them, so I agreed.
   In return, they agreed to wash our clothes.
   I don't think my husband would have minded,
     they just wanted to feel useful.
     He's a Levi's and t-shirts type of guy.
     He wears them like a Dior suit.
     He is perfect,

Purple Snowflakes

a prince.
My sense of style is slightly more multifarious.
She washes my things with what was once my favourite washing powder.
Apparently, it only comes in a plastic bubble full of goo now.

"Kids are eating it, so the box comes with a warning", she tells me. "I don't recall us being that crazy."

(You weren't.
You were wonderful;
everything around us was a disaster.)

But she does remember how I have three favourite brands of socks
and that I don't wear synthetic fabrics.
She remembers that I can't sleep on feather pillows,
that I can't fall asleep without a weighted blanket unless my husband is with me,
and that I never use fabric softener or dryer sheets.
All the laundry is neatly folded or hung and arranged in a similar fashion to the way I set up their closets as children.

Watching her makes me remember...all the shouting I did when I would try to find something in their messy closets.
At the time, I didn't understand things were symptoms,
once I did, I beat myself senseless from the guilt.

I remember the day I was told if I wanted to be part of my family again, I needed to "put clean socks on those kids."
I worked eighteen hours a day at the time.
I used to buy them new clothes constantly,
so people would think I was a good mother.
Washing all those clothes took an entire day's wages at the launderette.

I remember that I never use Tide because the man I was once married to was allergic to it.
I remember that I must never wash his uniforms until I check the pockets for pens.
I remember not being allowed to grieve when my babies died.
I remember when I was pregnant with this sweet girl who is putting away my collection of purple clothes,

and the Navy told him he was only required to give me forty some odd dollars every payday.

I remember when he left and did that.

I remember how God provided.

I remember the day I was finally able to forgive him for everything.

"You were never supposed to marry him in the first place," Holy Spirit reminded me. "Stop seeing everything through his lens."

I wrote him a letter and set us both free.

I'm able to commit the image of my daughter lovingly putting up my colourful clothing to my memory.

She doesn't slam the drawers.

She doesn't throw the empty hangers on the floor.

She doesn't huff or sigh.

She asks me while she works, hopeful that I might say something,

if I'd like new slippers;

if she should order me the harem pants she saw online;

if I would like some new bedding when she goes to the outlets.

She tells me she's going to ask my husband if the kids can go to work with him so she can do some early holiday shopping.

My girls call him their dad.
Every time they do, it fills my heart with joy, even though I don't say anything.
He's the only one they've ever known.
Jesus gave them the absolute best He had.

IV

Today feels like a threshold.

I'm taking in everything she does and says.
Hopefully, I will remember it again soon.

It's different every day.

    Last week, I spent nine hours remembering the kids who bullied me in grade school.
    Fifth grade in particular.
    I remembered their names, which houses they lived in, and what they looked like.
    I remembered how cruel they were, and how alone I felt.
    I remembered going to mass on Fridays.
    I loved it.
    I wanted to be a saint so that I could live a life devoted to God
        and walk in miracles.

I remembered junior high, and upperclassmen I didn't even know scrutinizing me terribly.

I remembered teachers who picked on me just because...

I remembered wanting to be a nun so I could spend all of my time with Jesus.

I remembered the devastation at finding out I couldn't do that because I wasn't Catholic.

I remembered wanting so badly for God to kill me,

that I was angry the first time I tried to do it myself and failed.

I forgave every one of those people as I remembered them.

I broke every soul tie and asked God to bless them and set them free.

I forgave my parents because it felt like they didn't protect me.

That was the day I fully forgave Him for allowing that season to be so horrible.

On March 12th, I began six hours of remembering my step-grandparents.

I met them when I was four years old.

41 Purple Snowflakes

I remembered the love they sowed into me,
how there was always encouragement and a push to be excellent that I didn't understand until years later.
I remembered how proud Grandpa was when I would write and win awards.
He would ask me about it when no one else was around,
and tell me I could be anything I set my attention to.
I remembered snuggling with him even as a teenager.
He never minded.
I remembered calling him from the hospital when I became a mother.
His voice was sweet and tender.
I had no idea he was so sick.
I remembered when he died, and I couldn't get home...

I remembered eating Special K with my Grandma in tiny melamine dishes.
She had a turquoise kitchen straight out of 1962.
I remembered how petite and elegant she was,
her hair and cosmetics always perfect,

walking home from the bus after work on high heeled shoes and her leather trench coat.
 I remembered how we would take the bus to downtown Montreal,
 Auntie Netta would style my hair before we had lunch.
 Grandma was always trying to teach me how to be a lady.
I remembered how I hated the pink dresses she liked in the shops – but not really.
I remembered how she'd make Scottish food when she visited,
how we shopped for treats at Marks and Spencer,
how she knit the best sweaters in the entire universe.
I remembered how tiny she seemed in the little flat in my parents' house,
how different she seemed without my Grandpa,
how sweet she was with my girls.

I remembered finding her prayer book from 1937,
how much peace I had when she went to Jesus even though it hurt.

My stepfather's parents were the light of my life from the moment I met them.
I realized that the only memories I have of them are good.

I remembered the day I met my Grammy Hilda.
She stood on her porch in the chilly December air and stretched her arms out.
My stepmom walked me to the house.
I was seventeen and nervous...
I'd just met my father for the first time since I was two.
I'd just met my little brother and my stepbrother.

"Oh, this must be my granddaughter!" she said with a beaming smile.
I stood two steps down while she hugged me.
I was her granddaughter; it was never a question.

I remembered the years after that, calling Hilda from England on Palm Sunday,
hearing her voice on the phone when the baby died,

going to lunch with her and hearing stories about how Wildwood used to be.

Mostly, I treasured how Hilda loved to go to the beach and hear the bugler at sunset,

how the parking spot at the flagpole was always empty just for her.

The girls and I used to take her after school.

And then...I remembered how my daughter was ridiculed in kindergarten for telling someone her Grammy fell out of an elevator and died.

I remembered going to the school and losing my religion in the office.

"We just lost our Grammy!" I shouted, "She fell stepping out of an elevator and died in surgery. Why would you treat my daughter that way!?"

I remembered after that how the police would follow my car until we moved,

and my girl was constantly picked on.

I remembered how my stepmom and father came from Florida for Hilda's funeral.

I remembered her radiant smile, how she rejoiced at her mother's Homegoing despite her sorrow.

45   Purple Snowflakes

 I remembered going with her to buy new shoes for work because I was doing so much overtime.
 How proud of me she was.
 How kind she was to the girls.
 I remembered how it warmed her heart to tell me how much Hilda loved spending time with the girls and me.
 I remembered how my girls loved her so much,
  and how she always said, "Jesus loves you; so do I!" every time she'd leave them.

 I remembered my father and how he sat in my kitchen more focused on the dishes in my sink than his grandchildren.
 I had just worked a twenty-hour shift.
 I remembered how he spent thirty minutes telling me about things he'd seen working for Children's Services.
 I remembered how proudly he told me about the mother whose kids he recently threatened to remove from her home unless she washed her dishes while he watched.

 I remembered how that was the moment I realized the man sitting at my table,

who knew what happened three hundred and seventy-one days prior,
 would never stop mentally abusing me.
 I remembered the day I stopped speaking to him to keep my peace.

 I remembered the day I forgave him and redeemed our soul ties.
 I remembered how free it felt.

Purple Snowflakes

V

Back in January, I spent eight days remembering scattered moments of joy, adventure, and labors of love.
So sublime.

I remembered the moment each of my girls was born,
    taking a ferry to Lewes in two countries,
    hiking at a volcano Park on Hilo,
    swimming with sea turtles on Oahu
    taking a bus across Norway,
    my sister-in-law and I singing karaoke,
    spending hours on the phone,
    making curry,
    pretending to be zombies in Evans City,
    and loving one another through divorce.

I remembered seeing my youngest daughter when I came home from the ICU,

screaming at Rick Emmet from the nose-bleed section,
   watching hockey in French with my Grandpa,
     foxtrotting with my Grandma,
     plastic Santa suits and green Gremlins.
   The way the snow fell in the Laurentians, and the first fabric painting I made in high school.

   I remembered that T-Rexes can't hug because they have tiny arms,
     Sailor Moon liked to eat a lot,
     and when you are six, adventure is everywhere.

   I remembered hearing my husband say my name for the first time,
     staying up all night praying with him,
     trying so hard not to be obvious while I gave him precious little gifts every day and
        hoping he didn't think I was daft.

   I remembered the first time he played the guitar for me,
     and how I could feel love radiating towards me... but I was so afraid to "read into it".

How it was so sacred a moment that I took a picture without him knowing.
So many moments with him were like that, are like that;
saturated with peace, love, and something just for me...
Our friendship pulled me so much deeper into the presence and peace of God,
It forced so many painful things out of my soul,
I hardly recognize who I was before I met him.

Although...
I remembered how I loved life and wanted to experience everything
when I was young,
and wanting that for my children.
Driving with the sunroof open and trips to Valley Forge,
picking wild blackberries on Skye and visiting castles in London,
just trying to make good memories for them when life was chaos.
Something good to pull from when you can't handle another hit.

VI

On my last birthday...all three of my girls came to see me.

I can go into the moment as though it's happening now.

They celebrate that I was born nineteen thousand seven hundred and ten days ago.

My youngest daughter just finished high school.

Her graduation pictures have come in the mail, and she is holding them up for me.

She sits across from me and puts one in my hand.

All three girls are in the picture,
beautiful as can be,
standing around someone who looks just like me.

I remember them coming and bringing what they said was my favourite dress,

arranging my hair in a bun,
painting my fingernails to match theirs.
My husband drove us to the graduation ceremony.
Parents who used to be my friends smiled sympathetically at him.
Teachers told me how I should be proud as though I might not be.
I remember my son in law taking pictures on four different devices.
I remember how happy they all were.
I was happy too; I just didn't say so.

It's the same now.
They smile as they bring me gifts and set them in my lap.
My middle girl opens the wrapping paper and lifts the box lid.
She tucks the Raggedy Ann and Andy dolls into my arms.

They remind me of my Grandmom,
one of the kindest people I ever knew.
I remember the Raggedy Ann and Andy dolls I had as a little girl,
how much I loved them,
how heartbroken I was when they were lost.

I remember my Grandmom and Grandpop's house, always warm and full of love.
I remember her tiny flat after my Grandpop died, always warm and full of love,
Raggedy Ann and Andy sitting on the bookshelf.
I remember taking my youngest girl to see her, the first and only time,
one Mother's Day when we happened to be back home after ten years.
How she had a moment of clarity and blessed my sweet girl.
I remember that she died that Thanksgiving.

My girls visit for a while before the grandbabies come in from a game of chase-Zeide-with-pool-noodles.

They've baked me chocolate cupcakes with raspberry frosting.
They say that it's my favourite, but I don't remember if I actually like cake or not.
My granddaughter sits on my lap with the cupcake most laden with raspberries on the top.

Purple Snowflakes

The rocking chair shifts, and she drops it, icing side down.

Raspberries splatter all over the hardwood floor.

She's sad that the best one was for me, Gusha, and it's gone.

My husband wipes her tears and helps her find another cupcake,

his voice so tender I close my eyes and remember the first time I heard it.

Her mother cleans it up and tells her everything is okay.

For the next week, I remember all the times I screamed and yelled over everything, including spilled milk.

I lay every moment at the foot of the Cross.

I watch Jesus redeem the time for my girls and me.

VII

Today still feels different...

I'm missing my husband terribly.
I'm asking God to bring him home soon so we can pray together.
Sometimes I hate it when he's not here.
Especially when the visiting nurse comes.
I'm sure he senses my distrust towards her; he always knows when I'm not peaceful.

Today she smells like my missing violet and melissa hydrosol.
She's wearing a very distinct colour of eye-shadow; the same colour my oldest daughter helped my husband find for me online.
It only comes from France.
It went missing last week when my sister-in-law asked to do my makeup.
She tells my daughter that I look nice,
and what a good day I had yesterday.

Purple Snowflakes

She tells my grandson how beautiful the snowflakes are.

Except that I remember yesterday...

She rolled her eyes when my grandson brought me the snowflake he'd made from a magazine picture.
Once my daughter went home, she told someone on her phone how ridiculous I am,
what an attention whore I am for "doing this" to my family.
She suggested that my husband probably doesn't work as much as he says he does.
She laughed at the easy money she was making from my midlife crisis.
When my husband arrived, she sweetly told him she was praying for me.

I remember all the times she turned off the music my husband leaves playing for me and played what she wanted.
I remember the times she ate my meals telling me that if I cared I'd say something.
I remember how she's picked through my jewelry box and tried on my rings,
dared me to tell anyone
that she's taking my favourite earrings.

I remember when she found the Turkish delight my kids gave me for Mother's Day and took it home with her,
how she told them she had no idea what I'd done with it.

I'm not even angry with her.
I remember leaving nursing three thousand six hundred and eighty days ago because of people like her,
because I couldn't pretend to not see them anymore.

Somehow my daughter knows...

She tells the nurse that she better hadn't find another chili-lime-flavored deep-fried pork rinds package in my wastepaper basket
unless it's a Kosher brand.
That if the music is changed one more time, she's going to send her a Spotify bill.
That if my tamanu, amla, and pomegranate oils with silk proteins, palm, and sulfate-free shampoo in the reusable bottle is not replaced by tomorrow, she is going to call the agency.
That if one more piece of all cotton, made-fair-trade-in-India, hand-dyed clothing goes

missing, she is going to put a camera in my closet.
    Wonder nurse sputters and stammers.

    My daughter tells her that she's had a second thought:
    if she ever sees her here again, she'll have her arrested for harassment.
    For all of my jewelry, missing clothing, books, trinkets...she and her dad are pressing robbery charges.
    "My dad has kept a list of everything you've stolen from my mother in the three weeks you've been here," she says. "He may be quiet, but he's not blind."

    The nurse looks like she's been slapped with a wet fish as my daughter escorts her out of the house.
    I think it's funny.

    My girl is a fighter.
    Thank God she is,
    I fought hard for her and her sisters even before they were born.
    Through the years of emptiness, the sadness, the despair,

I had enough hope and faith to go to the mattresses on every front for my girls.

Thank God they can fight for themselves now.

Thank God they have a dad who is a man of great faith.

Thank God, because I have no fight left in me.

Or perhaps my solitude *is* the last battlefront.

I am constantly, silently speaking with Holy Spirit.

VIII

When the nurse is gone, my daughter crouches down in front of me.

She smells like hibiscus and roses.

I remember that she always has since the day she was born.
I remember how her ten-year-old smile lit up a room and made the sun seem dim.
I remember when she was struggling,
how I always saw her victory rather than her victimhood.
I remember the day she realized it for herself.

"I know you're in there, Mom. I wish you'd come back," she says kissing my forehead.

I don't know that I'll ever come back.

I do know that I'm not completely gone.

It's more like a respite.
The field hospital of my mind was a violent mess.
My soul was full of shrapnel.
The triage was littered with these painful things that tried to kill me while Holy Spirit performed open-heart surgery.
Sometimes it's like prison being trapped in my head with anxiety and memories.
It's safe there, too.
No one can tell me how to feel.
It's a hermitage.

You see, it's been a long time coming, this time to get quiet.
It's frustrating having a photographic memory.
It's difficult to remember conversations verbatim, situations completely.
It's maddening when other people only have a selective recall.
It's a bittersweet process to walk with God, everything around me self-destructing.
Knowing the Man of Sorrows has been worth the cost, don't mistake me.
I just got tired.

I want to say, "Yes, babyness, I'm in here. I'm just resting."

But I can't.

All I can do is lean my forehead against hers.

I let her hug me.

I still love hugs.

Today is the one thousand nine hundred and fifty-third day since I stopped fighting.

The one thousand nine hundred and fifty-fifth day since I stopped tasting food.

The one thousand eight hundred ninety-third day since I completely stopped finding things funny.

The one thousand eight hundred and ninety-first day since I stopped wanting to.

The one thousand eight hundred and third day since I lost interest in my favourite films.

The one thousand five hundred and ninth day since I threw my mobile phone in the bin.

The one thousand two hundred and twentieth day since I lost interest in reading.

The one thousand two hundred and third day since I stopped driving.

The one thousand and fifteenth day since I stopped singing.

The eight hundred and twelfth day since I stopped writing.

Each event had a different trigger.
I remembered something,
shut down something,
but couldn't explain why.

I still can't.
I'm not sure I need to.

Last year, over Passover, I remembered the "time of *not* remembering".
I remembered what triggered that season,
but I couldn't remember exactly how many days ago that was.
I remembered becoming a recluse.
I remembered shutting everything out,
blocking out the things so I could process the traumas and get healed.
Fighting through Lupus brain fogs,
just trying to clear some mental space so that I could go to work and bring home my minimum wage paycheck.

There were years,
decades of my life that were blank.
People, events, seasons...

Purple Snowflakes

It was like they never existed in the first place.
I remembered how much easier it was to go through the motions then.
For me, at least.
I remembered how my older girls just sort of tried to find their way with a newborn baby sister.
She was pink and angelic.

There were four thousand seven hundred and seventy-seven days between her and my oldest girl,
who slept under her crib while I worked at night.
She was four thousand and nine days younger than my middle girl,
who was the first to see her at the hospital.
I remembered how hard I tried to make a life for the four of us.
I remembered how tightly I gripped Jesus' tzitzit during that time

But I also remembered wishing I could remember going to prom,
the first time I saw snow,
the last time I could trust anyone,
and who I was before my broken marriage.

I remembered how people on the internet knew me from high school,
 but I had no recollection of them at all.
 I hardly remembered my beautiful mother,
 besides a few specific snippets here and there,
 until I was about seven years old.

 I remembered thinking the memory lapse was because of a car accident.
 It very well might have been.

IX

And then a series of events uncapped everything.

My beautiful mother raised me, not my grandmother.
No; that was someone else's narrative to me as a child.

Good and bad memories trickled in.

There were rock concerts,
Bahamian vacations,
yachting with my grandparents in Quebec,
trips to the zoo,
a snowstorm in Dallas when I was ten,
hiking in Alaska at age sixteen,
high school dances and underage clubs in the city,
8track tapes and Van Morrison songs on a hillside with my mother in 1975.
OH! My mother...

I remembered the time when we were extremely poor.
The way she made corned beef hash from a tin,
how perfectly crispy it was,
how no one else has ever been able to get it right.
I remembered her reading poetry to me; she'd written it when I was a baby.
I remembered her long,
beautiful hair and doe brown eyes.
How we snuggled in bed when my stepdad worked nights,
how she taught me to bake cookies,
and the first time we heard "Grandma Got Run Over by a Reindeer" one Christmas while she was working.
I remembered going to the CN Tower,
to see "Wizards" in Montreal,
how the London YMCA looked like an ice castle when it caught fire one winter.

I remembered how she was always proud of me,
always telling people about my writing or my wonderful grades.

Then I remembered how horrible I was as a kid,
how I worried that she was still angry with me for being a mental wreck.

I remembered always feeling less than everyone else,
wondering why I was always angry,
wishing I had someone to talk to.
There was a flood of emotions I had not felt in decades.
Visions of people I'd bullied,
a girl who molested me,
boys who used me,
friends who betrayed me.
How all of that became familiar patterns that would follow me
and eventually my girls
for so many years.

I remembered the years pastors told me that I should stay with an abusive spouse because God hates divorce.
My friends said I was sinning because I had anxiety, because I was sad.
I remembered constantly feeling like I failed,

being unable to accept the very truth my faith is founded on;
    the unconditional love of Jesus.
    I mean, after all, my mental state was a sin in the eyes of the American church.
    I remembered how hard I fought to hold on to the joy of my salvation,
    the sanctity of my own life,
    and the grace that covered my flaws.

    I would ask, "Why would You want me if I'm so damaged?"
    He would tell me, "Because my blood is on the lintel of your soul."
    I would declare, "I am who God says I am!" until I could believe it.

    There was power in that,
    healing and freedom.

    By Shavuot, Pentecost, the void was full again.

X

It's a curious thing, though.
Every day I remember the moment I met my husband.

It's been two thousand two hundred and forty-six days since Jesus told me to, "Look at him."
"I am, Jesus. We're having a conversation."
"No. LOOK at him..."
So, I did.
The noise in my mind quieted and everything around me stopped.
My soul felt completely peaceful for the first time in my life.
I had to rely on Holy Spirit to get through the simple introduction.

I remember the night Jesus reminded me of everything he showed me about my other self.

It was a montage of images...
the first time I sketched him in high school,
through years of counterfeits who came
while I was hearing so clearly about him.
How Jesus so clearly spoke to me that my sweet friend was the one I'd been seeing,
praying for over the years.
How his sister asked me what God was showing me and I had no words.

I remember how my spirit calmed when he prayed for me,
my heart overflowed when we prayed together.
I remember how I could always feel how close he was.
I remember crying,
struggling to believe that I was worthy of such a sweet man of faith.
I remember telling God,
"If he is only ever my dearest, closest friend, I could die happy."

More than once a day I remember everything about him
and how I wrestled with loving him and God at the same time.
How my Adonai told me it was okay,

that this beautiful man would become my best friend.

I remember how his tenderness healed places in me that I forgot were broken.

His gentleness ministered to my whole family.

I remember the first moment I saw something just for me in his eyes.

Yes, even though I don't speak anymore, I live that moment every day.

Perhaps I had to get this quiet to truly understand him.

To understand God.

To understand myself.

To understand my children, my parents, my friends...

To be fully aware of Holy Spirit speaking to me.

To receive the gifts of sonship and salvation Jesus gave me.

To remember everything from the perspective of Heaven.

Every day I grow closer to that place in Him I long to dwell...

or maybe I've always dwelt there;

I just feel like a citizen now.

XI

    Today I'm wearing slippers shaped like Wile E. Coyote's feet.
    Except these are pink and sparkly.
    I love them; they make me smile inside.
    My son gave them to me for Christmas.
    Last week my grandson made me a snowflake out of paper the same colour as the slippers.
    He was proud.
    I probably was, too.
    The slippers don't match my clothes in any way,
    but I love that my husband found them in the closet for me this morning.

    I'm wearing a peach-coloured salwar,
    my youngest daughter picked it out on her mission to India.

Purple Snowflakes

    It has purple trim with woodblock prints of peacocks and little mirrors sewn into the hem.
    She told me peacocks were my favourite when she gave it to me.
    My husband loves the purple dupatta that goes with it.
    He calls it my mantle.

    It's been one thousand and six days since I cared about colours.
    I know that pink and purple were my favourites the day before that,
    but I can't remember why.
    I had a brown pair of slippers like these when I was a teenager.
    I wore them to cadet camp in Whitehorse.
    I remember forming up in the mornings wearing them,
    making people laugh.
    I remember doing things like that a lot,
    but I can't remember if I was actually funny or just weird and awkward.

    I remember the mountains,
    how it snowed on the mountaintop on my July birthday.
    I remember meeting my first boyfriend there.

I remember how I messed that up,
how he broke my heart,
how I squandered that entire experience.
I remember how I was searching for God at that time and mocking Him also.
I remember the day I asked Him to forgive me, and He did.
I remember going back to England fourteen years later and visiting that boyfriend,
how strong and honest our friendship had become over the years,
how lovely his wife and daughter were,
how much it healed my heart to be back in Devon by the sea with the girls.

My daughter is finished putting the laundry away and moving the snowflakes around.
She moves the date marker on the calendar and sets the music on a Hebrew playlist.
Habrera Hativeet; "Moroccan Wedding".
My absolute favourite song.
This I *do* remember.
When she was young, we danced to this music.
I remember believing the girls enjoyed it as much as I did.
I remember twirling in circles on the beach and raising my hands to Heaven.

Purple Snowflakes

    I remember feeling God all around me,
    thinking the girls were feeling Him, too.
    I remember the day I found out I had experienced that alone.

    I remember that was the day the rest of me died inside,
    but I kept that to myself.

    I remember the day I began to dance with Yeshua again.
    My bones freshly healed,
    dancing like David in a tent,
    proud to be a Jewess,
    surrounded by my covenant family.
    I danced to Habrera Hativit
    for the first time in over a decade.
    My Jesus and my darling were there.
    That was the moment He restored all of that Joy to me.

XII

I hear her phone ring.

"No, she hasn't said anything today. Yeah, we have an appointment at three. Dad's going to drive us in the truck."
I know she is speaking to her older sister.

They take me to a therapist in the city every three weeks.
My husband never misses an appointment.
He holds my hand while we wait and prays.
I often hear him in my spirit.
Knowing he is praying makes everything easier to walk out.
Sometimes he tucks me under his arm and plays with a stray lock of my hair.
He smells like sandalwood and frankincense.
Sometimes my clothes smell like roses and frankincense; he and I.

Purple Snowflakes

It is the most comforting thing...
I close my eyes and savor my favourite place to be;
anywhere as long as he is with me.

Every appointment seems to take forever.
It's always the same.

The nurse takes my weight and blood pressure.
She asks me about my medical history.
I never answer her, not a shrug, nod, or gesture.
Next, she huffs and asks whoever goes in with me on that particular day if there have been any changes in my "condition" since the last visit.
There never is.

She tells whoever is with me that they are not allowed in the session unless I want them there.
I always give them an obvious indication of what I want that day,
and they always make me feel safe.

I wait for the doctor for exactly thirteen minutes every time.

I sit in the chair facing the window
with my hands in my lap.
When he comes in, he clears his throat as though he's interrupted something scandalous and ceremoniously turns on a recorder.
He treats my husband with contempt because he will not let them commit me.
My beautiful husband just smiles and asserts his position.

I'm not sure what this man thinks is going to happen,
but he always asks me the same questions.
Sometimes I sigh and cast a glance his way just to challenge his arrogance,
Others, I play with my wedding ring or the hem of my sleeve.
He wants to be the one to make me talk; not the one to reach me, to understand why I stopped.

He has journal articles he's written on my "case" framed in his waiting room.
I suspect he assumes I can't read anymore, either.

"I don't know," I hear her say. "I don't think he's helped Mom at all. Neither does Dad."

Purple Snowflakes

No, he hasn't.

On our first visit, he told me to blink once for "no", twice for "yes".
I willed myself to keep my eyes open the entire time.
My eyes were dry for two days after.
On the second visit, he asked me why I felt like I needed his help.
I blinked once.
On another visit, he asked me why I felt I was entitled to special treatment.
I watched the traffic on the street outside his window.
Six busses went by that day.
When my mom came with us, he blamed her for my inability to cope with daily pressure which he felt caused my *psychosis*.
She cried.
I *accidentally* knocked over her double almond milk latte with vanilla and lavender syrup all over his desk.
Last month, he told me that if I wanted to get better, I needed to trust him.
I crossed my legs and memorized the number of squares on the air conditioner grate.
One hundred and sixty-eight.

My soul doesn't need him.

"Okay. I'm in their room putting up laundry. See you in a few."
She sits on the edge of the bed and tosses her phone to her left.
She studies the paper snowflakes.
I watch her face; I understand the frustration, the helplessness in her eyes.
I felt it for a long, long time.
I don't feel any of that anymore, even though I remember it.

Now there is only peace.

XIII

   No, I don't think about anything,
   just everything I remember.

   And for the last seven hundred and sixty-four days,
   every time I relive a memory,
   if it comes with pain, anguish, or self-punishment,
   I hand it over to Him.
   I wasn't able to do that before.
   Oh! How I wanted to let it all go and be free.
   I was too busy living for everyone but me.
   Too busy trying to maintain an excruciating façade to be able to get quiet and let God have everything.
   Until I met the one person I didn't have to hide anything from.
   Every moment before he found me has been or is being redeemed.

My cup is running over even if I don't tell anyone.

My grandson abruptly jumps up and runs from the room announcing that he needs to make another snowflake.
When he comes back with his lunch pail full of scissors, glue, and gel pens,
his mother watches him as he cuts the printer paper.
Fully concentrating,
his tongue poking out of the right corner of his lips,
he creates a delicate work of art.

All the while, he's singing, "Pictures of Lily made my life so wonderful...."
I taught him that song when he was six.

I remember cutting snowflakes as a child.
It was one of my favourite things to do.
I remember making them for a Valentine for my mom in second grade.
I painstakingly made every cut a heart and glued it to the belly of a man made entirely out of hearts.
He had accordion arms and legs, and a big, pink, heart head.

Purple Snowflakes

   I thought it was beautiful,
a masterpiece.
   My teacher, Mrs. Smith, said it was ugly.
   Of course, Mrs. Smith hated everything I did,
   but my mom loved it.
   I think she named him Fred.
   I loved making snowflakes.
   I spent hours at it.

   "Hey, big guy, what'cha making?" my oldest girl asks from the doorway.
   She already knows it could be a snowflake, a cartoon, or a story.

   "Gusha needed a snowflake that looks like a lily," he tells her as though she should have known.
   I wonder what it will look like if he decides I need one that looks like Boris the Spider.

   "Good idea," she agrees.
   In a few steps, she is sitting on my lap, kissing my cheek.
   She will never be too old for this.
   The floor creeks under the rocking chair.

   "Hi, Mommy."

It's been ten thousand two hundred and ninety-three and a quarter days since she made me a mother.

The most precious silence settles in the room, the only sound is my grandson singing on the floor.

When he's finished, he asks his mother to put the snowflake in the window.

"You and Aunt Doobie should make Gusha a snowflake, too, Mom!"

He delegates paper and scissors without waiting for them to comply.

"Why does she like snowflakes so much?"

My girls look at one another.

They tell him stories they've been told countless times about my childhood as they carefully cut.

About winters in the snow belt,

how snowshoeing and arctic camping was my favourite.

They remember how every time we moved to a different city,

it snowed on Christmas;

the winters were uncharacteristically wintery.

London, Houston, Oklahoma City.

They sing the "Snowflakes and Raindrops" song we loved from the dinosaur show I hated.

My youngest daughter joins us.
My husband has just brought her home from work.
He kisses the top of my head and tells me he loves me before he sits on the foot stool in front of me.
No one ever seems to mind that he positions himself this close to me.
Even before I began to shut down,
the girls just let it happen in the sweetest, most organic way.

I want to tell them all how much I am enjoying this moment,
but all I can do is appreciate the braid in my husband's hair.

Everyone talks about their days for a moment before my youngest girl changes the subject again.
She likes to hear the story about how the snowflakes in Helsinki were soft and downy.
As large as Pringles.

How they fell on her sister's cheeks and covered her nose.

I remember how snowflakes and snowmen always remind us of my youngest girl.

I remember how she used to love catching snowflakes on her nose and sledding for hours on end.

When she was a baby, we had a porcelain snowman music box.

It reminded me of her.

They have the same sweet smile.

It played "White Christmas" and wound with a key.

We wound the key so many times I memorized the body motion.

Eight and a half turns.

They remind her of the day they all dressed up like faeries and danced in the snow-covered back garden.

She wore a toddler-sized leather biker jacket.

I took an entire roll of pictures.

Three of those pictures are in frames on my dressing table.

I remember the first winter I knew my husband.

I asked him to paint me purple snowflakes.

Purple Snowflakes

When he gave them to me, they were so beautiful, I cried.

I'm still not sure why.

(That canvas is on the wall next to the window.)

It snowed on New Year's Day, one hundred and one days after I met him.

He sent me a text to tell me how he loved the weather.

I imagined him dancing in the snow with me.

It made me love him even more.

XIV

We miss the appointment.
No one mentions it.
I sense the unspoken agreement between my husband and our daughters...
The therapist is fired.
He was only taking me to appease them, anyway.

They tape their snowflakes to the window, using up the last free space.
It's the most beautiful thing I have ever seen.
My favourite people are all in this moment with me.
My other self is making a snowflake, too.
I feel this brand-new file opening in my memory...

But something more is happening.
Something sublime and wonderful.

My soul is content.
I mean...as completely content as it has ever been.
I need them to know.
It's been so long I almost gag...

"When your mom was your age," I say, my voice barely a whisper.
I never take my eyes off the window.
"Her and Auntie used to make snowflakes and put them in the front window.
They'd wear their pajamas inside out and when they woke up,
there was snow everywhere.
That winter the snow was up to her chest and the surf froze on the bay."

It's a good memory.
It was one thousand fifty-eight days after Children's Services appeared on my stoop and I realized we had no one.

We had Jesus.
He surrounded us.

We were moving on,
working out forgiveness.
Our friend came from England.

We spent four weeks praying,
traveling,
exploring the snow-covered Great Lakes,
the beach at home,
the Maritimes.
We ate whoopie pies while searching for moose and lobsters as we drove through Maine over New Year's.
It was God giving us a new start.
A new life that wasn't perfect
and still had heartaches,
but full of new friends and more of Him.

"When Little Auntie came home from the hospital on Christmas Eve,
it snowed for twenty minutes.
Houston doesn't get very much snow," I add.

My soul has clung to these tender memories.
But there is no self-criticism,
no lingering regret...
only the joy and wonder of the moments are relived as the images come to me.

My soul is in this moment now,
with no hint of sorrow or compunction.

Purple Snowflakes

   Joy is quietly bubbling within me.

   This is the miracle my sister-in-law always knew I would experience,
   the miracle I have been waiting a lifetime for...

   In my peripheral vision, I see my girls' reaction.
   They're smiling, silently hi-fiving one another.
   My youngest girl always loves to hear about when she was a baby.
   My husband has prayed for this moment, I know it.
   He smiles and touches my cheek.
   His eyes are full of something that is only for me.

   Seeing my husband in this moment with us...
   reminds me of poetry I wrote years ago.
   Poetry I wrote for him...before I ever met him.
   I'm glad they're all happy.
   I'm glad they don't make a fuss about me talking.
   It may not ever happen again.

My soul and I haven't decided.

"I forgot all about that," my daughter says.

I smile.

"Thanks, Mom," her younger sister says as she kisses me.
"Your hair looks nice today," my oldest daughter tells me after a long pause. "It's getting long. And more silver streaks."

"Like snow settling on it," my youngest girl agrees.

It's not that I needed more attention.
It's that I needed time to heal so I could become this person.
This gentle mother, wife, sister, daughter, friend.
I needed to be less turbulent so I could truly savor life moment to moment.

In fact, I wanted less attention, less action.
I was so haunted and overwhelmed by the time I stopped speaking,
I just wanted to leave the angry, stressed version of me behind.

Purple Snowflakes

"Make a snowflake with us, Gusha," my grandson insists.
It's important to him.
I can tell by the way he's holding the scissors and paper out to me.
"Make a new memory," is what he's really saying, even if he doesn't know it.

It's important to my girls too.
They watch him put the scissors in my hand,
curious about what I will do.

It's important to my husband,
simply because he loves me
and wants to see me set free.

It's important to me, I realize.
I want me to be set free, too.

It's been fifteen thousand nine hundred and fourteen days since I cut out a snowflake.
So...I slowly, deliberately make the little cuts in the paper – violet coloured paper – he's given me.
My soul goes back to that memory of making snowflakes for my mother,
of how we smiled,

of how much I loved the surprise of what happens when the paper is unfolded.
This time, I see my Redeemer with me there,
marveling at how creative, how sweet my imagination is.

I make little cuts for each of my children.
my babies in Heaven,
my stepdaughter,
my girls,
my husband's children – they are all mine.
There's a tiny diamond cut for each of my grandchildren,
Crescent slits for my moms and dad,
Another snip for my little brother,
my niece and nephew,
my grandparents,
my sister-in-law,
my brother-in-law,
the friends and precious people I have known in this life,
even my dog.

There isn't much space left to cut, but I'm not finished.

I make a circle in another piece of paper,

royal purple this time,
and fold it...
The center cut is for my Adonai.
Around that is something for my Jesus, and around that, a starting place for Holy Spirit.
I make small, perfect shapes for my husband
as I remember the moments when Holy Spirit showed me how my soul and spirit quieted when he was present.

Still another piece of paper,
a soft shade of lilac.
I fold it and shape it like a flower...

"Todah" I cut carefully.
Both English and Hebrew.
"Merci."
"Danke."
"Grazi."
"Thank you."
Because this small snowflake represents every moment,
every day that God counted
and kept His eye on me.
On my girls and grandchildren.
On my husband before we found one another.

All I can feel right now is gratitude,
thankfulness that He has done so much for me simply because He loves me.

This moment reminds me of the paintings and quilts I used to make in intercession.
Each time Jesus gave me a sketch,
He would say, "When you complete this, the matter is accomplished."
Some of those were difficult,
the breakthrough must have been intense.
Some went smoothly,
the declarations sweet and simple.
Each time, the matter was accomplished.
Every time my Adonai made a promise, He kept it.
He did more than I could possibly have imagined.

Because he knows where my thoughts are going,
my husband gives me the glue.
I layer the three pieces carefully.
Each one tells part of my story.
My oldest daughter hands the glitter over to me,
and I sprinkle the iridescent powder onto my paper creation.

Purple Snowflakes

Snow upon snow.
My purple snowflake.
It's beautiful.
It's like a kiss from heaven.
It's a cairn.
It's a mitzvah.
It's my mattah engraved with my history.
After all, God is rewriting my story.
Our story.
Everyone's story.
He is creating new narratives,
Changing plot lines and developing characters.

When I'm finished, my husband makes room for my delicate purple masterpiece in the center of the window.
On the other side of the glass,
the afternoon sun is gently slipping behind the birch trees.
Handmade windchimes and tattered snowflakes dance in the breeze.

That's why the rocking chair is in front of this window.
Birch trees are my favourite.
As a child they were all around me
I drew them constantly.

A few years ago,
we lived in the country.
There was a robin's nest in the birch tree outside the kitchen window.
Holy Spirit spoke to me through those birds for three years.
In Finland birch trees are everywhere.
They call it koivu and the oil of the tree is one of the most beautiful things...
I used to make soap from it.
When we bought the house,
my husband surprised me by planting birch trees outside our bedroom window.
They were a gift from my girls...to tell me we were all good.
I just couldn't receive it at the time.

Inside, the glitter sparkles as soft rays of light stream through.
Everything is gently overlapping,
stories intertwining.
It's a perfect collage.
Each snowflake reminds me of something.
Something good.
Something nothing else ruined.

My fluffy pink feet press the floor, and the chair begins to move.

Purple Snowflakes

Suddenly, I can't remember how many days it's been since I stopped rocking or why.

I can't remember how many days it's been since... anything that broke my heart.
I don't miss it at all.
God remembers it for me.
That's part of the easy yoke Jesus gave me.

Although I remember lovely things...
the days my grandchildren were born,
the week my parents spent with us last year,
how beautiful the sunrise on the inlet back home is,
the first time my husband held my hand...
the way he's holding it now.
My soul would rather be in this moment.

"Gee, ain't life sweet?" I sing softly.

Philippians 4:8 (TLV)

⁸ Finally, brothers and sisters, whatever is true, whatever is honorable, whatever is just, whatever is pure, whatever is lovely, whatever is commendable—if there is any virtue and if there is anything worthy of praise—dwell on these things.

101 Purple Snowflakes

Write about it...

    I want to encourage you to press on through every heartbreaking moment. If you ever feel as though no one understands what it is to constantly run into walls, climb the grease pole, or find yourself in the middle of drama when all you're trying to do is get around the last catastrophe, please know that you're not alone. I understand and so does Jesus. Some days you're doing great if you can brush your teeth and change your socks.

    Sometimes it feels as though reaching a breakthrough is near to impossible. I mean, until two years ago, I had all but forgotten who I really was. I was treading water while trapped in my thoughts as I relived decades of chaos, turmoil, and heartbreak. I watched my family break down for so many years, my soul was fractured, and my mind couldn't process anything more.

I knew the Lord. I had been in relationship with Jesus since age three.

I had, at one time, been so overwhelmed by the desire to seek and serve God, that while I was walking in miracles, generational destruction was wreaking havoc on my children. I was just beginning to walk out the revelation Holy Spirit gave me about breaking generational curses and dwelling in the Glory when I experienced a terrible deception, made unwise decisions, and found myself making another lap around the desert.

At nine years old I began to write poetry and songs to the Lord. By the time I was twelve, I was suicidal, and writing had become a therapy. Over the last thirty-eight years, it became my safe place, my sacred place with the Lord. Writing became my passion. It still is.

As I've been putting together this series called "Embrace", I've been finding old journals and chat files. I realize now that I was scribing my intercession, petitions, complaints, thanks, decrees to the One who treasures them. Holy Spirit has been reminding me where we were and who I was before everything fell apart at the seams: I was on fire.

Absolute consecration is required for the walk I'm called to. To navigate the road I've chosen.

Is it any wonder the winepress hurt so much?

As I've been editing and preparing this particular short fiction for publication, so much in my life has been stirred up. It's as though God has given Raphael the nod to trouble the waters in my pool. The aftermath of so many years of chaos, struggle, pressing in, crying out, and holding on to the tzitzit of my Jesus have become a powder keg. Light is exposing what is in the shadows and I am seeing promises come to pass before my eyes.

And yet...I am beside still, calm, tranquil waters with my Shepherd.

I want to encourage you in three things:

- ❖ Know Jesus and follow hard after Him.
- ❖ God is for you, even when He feels far away.
- ❖ You have survived every bad day you've ever had because there is a purpose and plan for your life.

If you have never made a decision for Jesus, you can be confident of this one truth; He has made a decision for you. This means He will always actively pursue you, no matter where your life is. He is always listening for your footsteps, for your voice to speak His name, for your soul to cry out to Him. He is waiting for you to take a drink of the Living Water and spend eternity with Him.

And it's so simple. You just tell Him that you need him, that you want a relationship with Him, that you surrender to His unrelenting Love for you. Then the most amazing adventure begins.

Purple Snowflakes

The closer you get to the Lover of your soul, the deeper into the mysteries of God you go. Your whole perspective changes because you are positioned with King Jesus in Heavenly places. From that place, you are able to look at every situation, past, present, or future, with the mentality of a child of God.

Over the years, God has felt very far from me. Some of that was because of my daddy issues, and some of those moments were purely a result of me letting temptation become sin...and everything that follows. Regardless of why I found myself there, my Adonai's desire was to see me victorious over my circumstances and free from every lie, sickness, sin, and iniquity.

My outlet has always been writing. Words are so very important. We live on torah after all. In the darkest nights of my soul, I wrote out psalms and prayers. I wrote letters to the one God has for me, just to keep myself from developing soul ties with the wrong man. I drafted characters, worlds, and plot lines based on what I was going through, where I was, who was around me. I poured my emotions into writing in some form or fashion, and I watched myself survive every calamity. I watched myself grow with each victory.

In every character, situation, and resolution, there is a piece of me. There is something of the nature of Jesus, of spiritual warfare, of intercession, of my destiny. I scribed it all. Holy Spirit is in every word.

Scribe your story. Prophesy your victory. Bring down your destiny from Heaven. Write it out. Write about it. Make every declaration over your life until you see the breakthrough. Dive into scripture and find your promise, your thesis statement. Write down everything as Holy Spirit speaks to you, because every word will bring you closer to your breakthrough.

Every breakthrough will bring you closer to your destiny.

Don't stop there! Keep scribing your songs of thanksgiving. Keep praising and declaring your victory. Keep exalting the Lord. And above all else, keep casting down every thought that wants to raise itself above your perspective as a child of God.

Purple Snowflakes

Sometimes you need to get quiet so you can stay in that mental place of revelation and calm while the chaos carries on around you. When you do, you hear Him so much more clearly.

Write about it, my friend. You will be glad you did.

h.e. newell 108

109   Purple Snowflakes

Other titles by the Author

The Beautiful Garbage

Frequency Sixteen

He Sets a Table for Me Before My Enemies